RAGGEDY ANN
and the
GOLDEN RING

RAGGEDY ANN
and the
GOLDEN RING
by Johnny
Gruelle

A YEARLING BOOK

Published by
Dell Publishing Co., Inc.
1 Dag Hammarskjold Plaza
New York, New York 10017

ISBN: 0-440-47331-4

Reprinted by arrangement with The Bobbs-Merrill Company, Inc.
Printed in the United States of America
Second Dell Printing—March 1978

CHAPTER 1

RAGGEDY ANN and Raggedy Andy were walking through the deep, deep woods in search of more adventures. The sunshine streamed down through the branches of the evergreen trees in ribbons of golden light and the birds sang and twittered happily in the leafy branches.

"The deep, deep woods are so lovely," Raggedy Ann said as she stopped to kiss a blue flower bending low on its green stem.

"And we have had such happy adventures here," Andy added.

Now one of the nicest things about the deep, deep woods is the magic that seems to bloom and grow there. Of course, many grown-up people never know of the magic of the woods. But most children do. And the Raggedys, with their shoe-button eyes, their cheerful smiles and happy hearts, were always able to see fairies, gnomes, elves, and magical things. That is why it was always easy for them to find a magical soda-water fountain, or an ice-cream mud puddle, or

a clump of pie plants, or any number of other wonderful, strange things.

So the Raggedys had gone only a short distance when they came to a lovely soda-water fountain which bubbled up from a large stone and then splashed down in a small, tiny fall to other stones below.

Whoever had made the soda-water fountain had also made some little silver cups with which to catch the soda water. The Raggedys sat down beside the bubbling soda-water spring, filled a silver cup and then enjoyed the ice-cold sodas.

"It is very pleasant to find a magical soda-water fountain after a long walk," said Raggedy Andy.

Raggedy Ann, her mouth full of soda, could only nod her head up and down. A moment later, the Raggedys were quite surprised to hear a tired voice say, "Please may I have a drink of the soda water? I'm a carpenter and I'm very, very tired."

There before them stood a bald-headed man whose shoulders and head, and even his smile, seemed to be drooping from tiredness. He was dressed neatly in

a carpenter's overalls, and in one pocket was a large hammer. Stuck here and there to his shirt and trousers were chips and small pieces of freshly cut wood.

Raggedy Andy could see how very tired the poor man looked and quickly gave him a silver cup full of the sparkling soda water which made the man feel ever so much better.

"Thank you so much," the nice carpenter said. "I was so thirsty!" So Raggedy Andy gave him six more silver cups of soda water.

But just as he finished drinking the soda water, a queer little man ran toward them shouting, "Here, give that to me! I'm just as thirsty as you are!"

And with that, he grabbed the cup of soda out of the carpenter's hand. For a moment, Raggedy Ann, Raggedy Andy and the tired carpenter stood speechless, for not only was the little man strange-looking, but he was very, very rude.

Then Raggedy Ann in her kindly voice said, "You did not have to grab the cup. If you had asked for it and said, 'please' we would have shared the soda with you gladly."

Raggedy Andy added, "But since you acted that way, I do not think we want to let you have any soda."

At this the little man's red face became even redder, and he shook his fist as his voice boomed, "I shall tie you up and then I will be able to have all the soda myself!"

But as he started to take some rope out of his pocket, the little carpenter stepped in front of the Raggedys and declared, "I will not let you harm these two nice rag dolls! They have been kind and generous to me and I can tell by their smiles that they are good little folk."

"Who are you?" the little man asked.

"I am the tired carpenter," the carpenter replied as he took a hammer and some nails out of his pocket. "And what is your name?"

"I am Toofie, and I shall let the Raggedys go and then I shall capture you," the queer little old man howled, "for I need a nice house and you can build it for me!"

"All right," the carpenter agreed, "but first I must find out how high your house must be to fit you. Just stand here while I measure you."

So Toofie stood upon a log and, before he knew what happened, the tired carpenter nailed both of Toofie's shoes to the log.

"Now," he said, as he gave Toofie a thump, "whenever you want anyone to do something for you, ask him in a nice manner."

Then he lifted Raggedy Ann and Raggedy Andy to his shoulders, picked up his tool box and walked

away through the woods.

"I shall show you the nicest patch of chocolate cream candies in the whole wide, wide woods," the carpenter said.

And in a few minutes, he set the Raggedys down gently. There they were right in the center of a large clearing in the woods and all around them were chocolate cream candies, growing on short stems and wrapped in tin foil.

"You fooled old Toofie, the queer little man, when you nailed his shoes to the log," Raggedy Ann said to the kind-hearted carpenter as she and Raggedy Andy licked the chocolate-cream candies.

"I surely did." The tired carpenter laughed. "I shall not let old Toofie capture you, nor shall I build him a house when he is so unpleasant and disagreeable."

"I guess Toofie will stand there with his shoes nailed to the log for a long, long time," Raggedy Andy said. "Maybe we had better go back and pull out the nails so that he may run home."

"Oh no!" the tired carpenter said. "If we do that,

Toofie will try to tie us up or something to make us do what he wants."

"But think how tired Toofie will get standing on the log for years and years," Raggedy Ann objected. "And he will get very, very hungry."

"Oh no, Raggedy Ann and Raggedy Andy," the tired carpenter assured them. "After he stands there awhile, Toofie will realize that only his shoes have been nailed to the log. When he unties his shoes, he will be able to walk right away."

And that is exactly what happened. For a few moments after the Raggedys and the carpenter left him, Toofie screamed and yelled as loudly as he could. But when no help came, he looked about him to see how he could help himself. Looking down at his feet, he suddenly realized that all he had to do was untie his shoelaces. And as soon as he had loosened his shoes, Toofie was off in a flash to find the Raggedys and their friend.

When he caught a glimpse of them through the trees, he stood very still while he took a little box from his pocket. Carefully he opened the box to make sure that his magic powder was still in it. With a sly little smile on his red face, he crept up behind the tired carpenter. Then when Toofie was directly behind the carpenter, he opened his box and blew some of the magic powder over the shiny bald head.

When the Raggedys saw the puff of powder floating over the carpenter's head and heard Toofie's mean laugh ringing through the woods, they knew he had worked some magic on their friend.

So Raggedy Ann and Raggedy Andy ran into the bushes and hid, for they were certain the tired carpenter would be captured. And, if they were to help the carpenter, they must get out of the path of the magic powder. So they stayed where they could watch the mean Toofie while they made some plans. They could see Toofie tie a string to the carpenter's nose and lead him away through the woods. All this time, the carpenter said not a word, and almost seemed to be asleep with his eyes wide open.

"He is taking him home and will make the carpenter build a house," Raggedy Ann said. "What shall we do, Raggedy Andy?"

"We can follow them and see what Toofie does with the tired carpenter; when we have a chance, we can rescue him," Raggedy Andy answered.

So the Raggedys quietly followed Toofie as he led the carpenter to a tiny house with a broken-down roof. In front of it stood a large tree to which Toofie tied the carpenter with a very long rope.

Then he said, "Now while I go inside my house and take a nap, you can build a nice little house for me because I am tired of living in this old house."

So Toofie went inside and the carpenter got out his hammer, nails and other tools. In a few minutes Toofie's loud snores could be heard outside.

Then the Raggedys slipped up and whispered, "Mr. Carpenter, we have come to rescue you. Take your knife and cut the string Toofie tied around your nose. Then we'll all run and leave Toofie fast asleep in his house."

At the sound of the Raggedys' voices, the tired carpenter seemed to awaken. He shook his head as though to clear the cobwebs from it.

Then he laughed and asked, "Where am I?"

The Raggedys put their fingers to their mouths, warning him to be quiet, and then told him what had happened. Once more, Raggedy Ann told him to cut the string and the carpenter did as Raggedy Ann suggested and was free. Then he took sticks and nailed them across Toofie's house so that when the little man awakened, he would not be able to get out of the house.

The Raggedys and the carpenter laughed softly as they ran off through the deep, deep woods.

They ran and ran until they came to a lovely tree with soft, golden biscuits hanging from each branch. And near by was an apple-butter mud puddle.

So they stopped and picked biscuits which they spread with the fine apple butter. What a fine picnic they had! And Toofie did not come along to spoil their fun for he was still sound asleep, nailed up in his little home.

When Raggedy Andy and the tired carpenter and Raggedy Ann had eaten as many of the rolls and apple butter as they wished, Raggedy Ann washed Raggedy Andy's and the carpenter's faces.

Then she said, "Now where shall we go? I guess old Mister Toofie will never be able to get out of his house, for you nailed the sticks very tightly."

"I think after a while he will break the sticks and then he will come after us once more and try to capture us," Raggedy Andy said.

"No, he won't!" The tired carpenter laughed. "Because I put three nails in the ends of each stick and the sticks are very strong. Toofie will not be able to break them."

"Why then," Raggedy Ann said, "it would not be right for us to go away and leave Toofie shut up inside his house. Think how we would feel if someone nailed sticks over our windows so we could never, never get out! Toofie will be very, very hungry! He has always been such a mean little fellow that I do not believe anyone will visit his house to bring food to him."

At this, the tired carpenter began to cry, for he had a very tender heart.

"Oh dear," he sobbed, "what shall we do? If we run away and leave him, Toofie will grow very thin and hungry. If we return and let him out, he will work his magic on us. What shall we do?"

Raggedy Ann wiped the tired carpenter's eyes with her pocket hankie and said, after thinking very hard, "Maybe, if we take a lot of these rolls spread with apple butter to old Toofie, he will feel so grateful that he will promise not to bother us again."

So the three friends buttered many of the rolls with the apple butter from the apple-butter mud puddle and ran back to Toofie's home.

Sure enough, there they found the queer little man pulling at the sticks which the carpenter had nailed across the window and roof and door, while he howled ever so loudly. All around Toofie's house, the little woodland creatures had gathered to see what the trouble was, but they did not offer to help Toofie.

"We have come back to help you, Toofie," Raggedy Ann said as she handed Toofie a roll through his barred window. Toofie was very glad to get it, for he was very, very hungry.

"Did you bring any more rolls, Raggedy Ann?" Toofie asked, his mouth full of food.

"Yes, Toofie," Raggedy Ann said. "You must stay there and eat them, for if we let you out of your home, you would puff your magic powder on us and put us to sleep or change us into toadstools or something."

"Not if you give me a lot of the nice rolls, Raggedy Ann. I promise," Toofie said very earnestly.

So Raggedy Ann made Toofie promise, "Honest to goodness, cross my heart!"

When Toofie had done this, the tired carpenter took all the sticks down.

"Thank you," Toofie cried. "Now give me the rolls and I promise never to work magic on anyone again, unless it is nice magic."

Raggedy Ann gave Toofie all the rolls, and the

tired carpenter said, "Now that Toofie has promised to be kind, I will build him a little house."

While Toofie was busy eating roll after roll, the carpenter took out his hammer and saw and nails. He was ready to start work when he stopped and stared straight ahead.

Suddenly he gasped, "Oh, my, look!"

He pointed with a trembling finger to a tree which had sprung up just beside him.

Now this was not an ordinary tree, no indeed! For hanging all over its branches, like lovely shining flowers, were glittering golden rings that shone brightly in the sunlight!

The Raggedys looked at each other and smiled happily while the tired carpenter and Toofie gazed at the tree silently. The Raggedys knew why the tree had appeared and what it meant. But of course Toofie and the tired carpenter could not know.

Excitedly, they asked, "Raggedy Ann, Raggedy Andy, where did this come from? Why is it here? Will it hurt us? Is it magic?"

WORTH GRUELLE

CHAPTER 2

THE RAGGEDYS were smiling so happily that Toofie and the carpenter instantly knew nothing could be wrong. But they were just as puzzled as they had been at first, so they asked question after question.

Raggedy Ann laughed and said, "If you stop asking questions, I shall tell you all you want to know."

Then when all was quiet, Raggedy Andy began, "Some time ago, Raggedy Ann and I had an adventure with beautiful Queen Matilda, and a prince and princess in the Snow White Castle. It is too long a story to tell you now, but you must know that before we left the Snow White Castle, kind Queen Matilda gave Raggedy Ann a golden ring just like the ones on this tree."

Toofie and the carpenter looked at Raggedy Ann who explained, "I gave the ring to the princess as a wedding gift, but before that I made a wish with it. The wish was that upon every spot where Raggedy Andy and I had an adventure, a tree would grow and hundreds of shiny magical golden rings would grow

16

on every branch. Then whenever anyone with a kindly heart came along, he could shake the tree and have a magical golden ring of his own. And he would have good luck with him as long as his heart was generous and kindly."

The carpenter and Toofie were beginning to understand, but Raggedy Andy thought he would make it very clear. "Because the carpenter has shown what a kind heart he has by offering to make a house for Toofie," he said, "the golden ring shall be his."

So the carpenter shook the tree and a lovely, perfectly round golden ring fell down from a branch and lay at the carpenter's feet. As Raggedy Andy stooped to pick it up, he frowned for a minute.

Then he said, "Mr. Carpenter, you do not seem to be tired any longer. What has made you change?"

The carpenter put the ring on his middle finger, threw his head back and straightened his shoulders as he laughingly replied, "You are right, Raggedy Andy, I am not tired. But I do not know why I have changed. Anyway, I think I had better start on Toofie's house if I am to get it finished soon."

He picked up his tools and the wood he planned to use and, whistling happily, started his work. And very soon, the little house began to take shape.

"How did you happen to become a tired carpenter?" Raggedy Ann asked as he made the front door of the cozy little house for Toofie.

"Oh, I don't know," the carpenter replied. "I remember that when I was a little boy, I never liked to do the things my mother asked me to do. So, of

course, when I grew up, I had the habit of letting someone else do the things I should have done. I guess I was tired because I did not do very much."

Raggedy Andy nodded his head. "It is just as easy to be tired from doing nothing as from doing too much."

"You must have been a lazy boy," Toofie said.

"That is so," Raggedy Ann agreed. "But, Mr. Carpenter, you do not seem to grow tired now from building the nice house for Toofie!"

"Oh, my, no!" The carpenter laughed. "Maybe it was Toofie's magic powder. Or perhaps my tiredness left me when Toofie tied the string around my nose."

Toofie laughed. "Maybe it would be a good plan for all mothers to tie strings around the noses of their little boys who are too tired to help."

"Now I shall go back home and go to work," the carpenter said as he nailed the last board down on Toofie's house. "For I am not a bit tired!"

"I know what to do," Toofie said to the carpenter. "You stay here and live with me in my nice little house. Then I shall use my magic to make boards and nails and you can build darling little houses for the woodland folk who now have to live down under the cold stone in the musty ground."

"Hmm." The carpenter thought. "I think that would be lots of fun, Mr. Toofie."

"How much shall I have to pay you a day?"

"My goodness," the carpenter replied, "if I live with you here in your nice little house and eat the nice things you serve from your magic cupboard, I won't need any money."

"Then you shall stay," Toofie cried as he gave the carpenter a pat upon the back. "We shall start right away to build little houses. Then I will take them in my wheelbarrow and give them to the tiny creatures."

"Why not just build a city of tiny houses right here?" Raggedy Ann asked. "You could be the mayor, Toofie, and the carpenter could be the chief of police and the town carpenter too."

"Wheee!" the carpenter and Toofie both cried as they caught hold of Raggedy Ann's hands and danced about. "That is just what we will do!"

At that moment there was a weak little tap on the front door and when Toofie opened it, a little field mouse, dressed in ragged clothing, asked, "Please sir, will you give me a few crumbs to take home to my sweet mouse-wife? She is ill in our home down under an old damp log."

"There, you see!" Toofie exclaimed. "We must get right to work, for here are two sweet little mice who need our help."

So Toofie with his magic charms made a lot of boards and nails and said, "Now while Raggedy Ann and Raggedy Andy take a basket of food over to Freddy Field Mouse's home, Mr. Carpenter and I will build them a nice little dry house."

So he handed the Raggedys a basket of food and with Freddy Field Mouse leading the way, the Raggedys soon came to the Field Mouse home beneath the damp log. Freddy Field Mouse took the basket of food down to Mrs. Field Mouse and when he came up a few minutes later, his mouse-wife was with him.

"The food tasted so good, I think it must have been magic food," Mrs. Field Mouse squeaked. "I would like to go back with you and thank Mr. Toofie myself."

So the Freddy Field Mouses, Raggedy Ann and Raggedy Andy all ran back to Toofie's house where the carpenter had just hammered in the last nail on a tiny house. Toofie, with a pot of paint in one hand and a paintbrush in the other, was about to start his painting. Mr. and Mrs. Freddy Field Mouse were delighted with the little house for it was just their size

and was furnished with a little table and chairs and two little white beds.

"When I have finished painting, we will build some more houses," said Toofie.

"Hurrah for Toofie, the kind little magician!" Raggedy Andy cried, catching Toofie's hands and dancing him all around the little house.

Raggedy Ann's shoe-button eyes danced and twinkled happily too, for Toofie and the carpenter had built twenty-five tiny, sweet houses which were all for the little homeless woodland creatures.

Toofie's house itself was just large enough for Toofie and Mr. Carpenter and now it was the center of a little town, surrounded by the teeny houses they had built. And, of course, next to Toofie's house was the lovely tree with the golden rings hanging from it.

"Now we must find the little woodland creatures to live in the houses," Toofie said. "So I shall work my magic to tell all the creatures who need cozy homes to come to our tiny town."

Taking his magic charms, he faced first to the north, then to the south, then to the east and then

21

to the west, as he sang, "Higgledydiggity, now let them run! Higgledydiggity, now let them come! Right here to Tiny Town! To houses of their own!" Then he added, "Hocus Pocus!" and kicked up his heels to finish the magic charm.

And in a few moments, the Raggedys and the carpenter and Toofie all heard the sound of tiny feet pattering toward them, as well as many squeaks and much laughter.

"Here they come!" Toofie cried excitedly.

And sure enough, the woodland creatures came in droves—Mama Woodchuck and her Woodchuck twins, Mrs. Weasel and Mr. Walter Weasel, Theresa Hoppytoad and six little Hoppytoads, Grandma and Grandpa Hootieowl, who were tired of living in an old musty hollow tree, Lawrence Lizard and Lena Lizard, Katy Cottontail and Karly Cottontail and their bright family of little bunnies, and hundreds of other little woodland creatures.

When they had gathered around and looked in all the doors and windows of the little teeny-weeny houses, there were many excited squeals. Everyone

admired the houses so that they all wanted to live in Tiny Town and have Toofie for the mayor.

"But dear me!" cried Toofie when he saw so many woodland creatures. "There are not one-half enough houses for all the creatures who are here, and there are sure to be more coming soon!"

Even as he spoke, more little woodland creatures came running up, crying, "Are we too late? Are we too late?"

Toofie shook his head sadly and replied, "I am afraid you are! I did not expect so many of you would want new houses. The carpenter and I have built all we can build today, for I am sure Mr. Carpenter is very tired."

"Not a bit," cried Mr. Carpenter excitedly, as he rolled up his sleeves. "If you will make more boards and nails with your magic, Mr. Toofie, I will soon build many more houses."

"But even if you build the twice as fast as you built them before, we shall never be able to catch up with all the creatures who are coming," Toofie said.

Then he turned to Raggedy Ann who had been sitting on the roof of a tiny house, thinking very, very hard, but saying nothing. "What shall we do, Raggedy Ann?" he asked.

"Well," said Raggedy Ann, running her rag hand up through her yarn hair, "if you cannot build the houses fast enough for the little homeless creatures, why don't you take your magic charms and wish for each house to be already built, just the size for the creature who needs it?"

Toofie gave Raggedy Ann a hug and cried, "Hurrah for Raggedy Ann! That is just what I shall do! And I will wish for a nice little soda-water ice-cream parlor too, where everything will be free."

In a few minutes, the little magician had done all he had said and even more. He built a meat market and a grocery store too, so that everyone might have all the food and goodies they wished for.

"Isn't it a fine little town, Toofie?" Raggedy Ann asked, watching the little magician's eyes sparkle.

"Indeed it is, Raggedy Ann! But there is one thing that worries me," Toofie replied.

"What is that, Toofie?" Raggedy Ann asked.

"Well, you know," Toofie answered, "the carpenter was a tired carpenter before he built my house and all these other houses for the woodland creatures. But since then he has had nothing to do and I am afraid that if he has nothing to do, he will soon become tired and dissatisfied again."

"That may be true, Toofie," Raggedy Ann nodded. "Whenever a person has nothing to do, he becomes lazy and discontented."

Just then Raggedy Andy said very seriously, "Toofie, Mr. Carpenter here says he believes he will leave Tiny Town and go out into the world again, for there is nothing more for him to do here."

"Yes," the carpenter said. "I am growing tired again, Mr. Toofie!"

"This will never do," Toofie cried. "I shall get my charms and make your tiredness disappear!" And off he ran to his little house.

"I know what would be even better, Mr. Toofie!" Raggedy Ann cried when Toofie came out of his house with his box of magic charms. "You should find something for Mr. Carpenter to do. Then he won't feel tired. People never do feel tired when they are doing something useful."

"But I do not know how to do anything except carpentry work," the carpenter objected sadly.

"Why not build a fine large grocery store with a meat counter and fruit and vegetable stands as well as a bakery corner? Then the carpenter could be the Tiny Town grocery man," Raggedy Andy suggested.

"But Toofie has already built a tiny grocery store and meat market," Raggedy Ann said.

"That won't make a bit of difference," Raggedy Andy replied, "because every town has more than one grocery store and meat market. And Tiny Town has so many creatures living in it now that they really need more than one grocery store."

"That is so," Toofie said. "How would you like to be the grocery man, Mr. Carpenter, and you can wait on all the little creatures and wrap their packages for them and everything?"

"I have always wanted to be a grocery man." Mr. Carpenter laughed.

So Toofie built a very large grocery store with his magic and Mr. Carpenter took charge with a big white apron tied around his middle. And, very soon, the new grocery man, all smiles, waited upon the tiny woodland creatures who were his first customers.

C H A P T E R   3

"Now I BELIEVE you have the finest little Tiny Town
in all the world, Mr. Toofie," Raggedy Ann said to
the little magician who with his friend, Mr. Carpenter, had built hundreds of little houses for the woodland creatures.

"I think so too, Raggedy Ann," Toofie said as he
helped the Raggedys to chocolate-covered cookies
from the Tiny Town grocery store. "And the nice
part of it all is that Mr. Carpenter is happy living
here with me and running the grocery store."

Mr. Carpenter was busy arranging the shelves and
putting things in order. And the Raggedys and Toofie
stood in the magic grocery store and drank bottles
of ice-cold pop and ate cookies.

Suddenly a little fat man with a long nose came
walking in and said, "Who told you that you could
build a town and a grocery store here? These are my
woods and I don't allow anyone to clutter them up
with little houses and stores. I shall tear them all
down and burn them up!"

Raggedy Ann, Raggedy Andy, Mr. Carpenter and Toofie all stared at the fat man with the long nose. He was so very fat that if his nose had not been so long, it would have looked like a button on his fat face. And although his words were most unpleasant, even a little scarey, they could not help but giggle, for the fat man was so funny-looking.

Raggedy Ann was the first to remember that it is not good manners to laugh at a person because of the way he looks.

She stopped giggling and asked, "Who are you? What is your name?"

"I am Dinkie," replied the fat man loudly, "and I own these woods. These little houses do not belong here so I shall tear them down as I said before."

"But the houses are for the poor little woodland creatures who have to live in stuffy trees and down under cold stones unless they can live in these cozy little houses," Raggedy Ann protested.

"I do not like any of the little creatures," the fat man howled. "I want them to move out of my woods."

"Dear me," Toofie said, "what a disagreeable person!"

Then he said to Dinkie, "You should be glad the little creatures live in your woods, for they are kind and happy all the day long."

"Out they must go!" Dinkie cried. "And all of you must go too. I won't have a grocery store here!"

And he began pushing Raggedy Ann and Raggedy Andy and Toofie out of the grocery store. He had pushed them as far as the front porch when Mr. Carpenter, who had been wrapping some packages for the Bunnikin family saw what was going on. And being very strong, he ran out and took the little man by the collar, lifted him up in the air and shook him.

"Here now," Mr. Carpenter said calmly, "you can't come into this magic store and push everyone around."

And he gave Dinkie a cuff on his ear as he put him on his feet again. The little fat man howled ever so loudly, just as a new puppy dog does when he is shut up in the basement the first night.

"He says that he owns this great big large woods," Raggedy Andy told Mr. Carpenter.

"I don't believe a word of it." Mr. Carpenter laughed. "He will have to prove to us that he owns this woods. So if he knows what is good for him, he will run home as fast as he can."

"I'll come back and break up all the little houses for kindling wood!" Dinkie cried. "Then I shall take the grocery store with its magic ice-box and everything for my own, and I shall live in Toofie's house."

But Mr. Carpenter just laughed again, "Ha, ha, ha!" as he ran after the little fat man and gave him a thump on top of his head which sent his hat down over his ears. "If I ever catch you here again bothering anyone, I will hit you twice as hard!"

And Dinkie, the little fat man, shaking with anger, ran away through the woods promising in a loud voice that he would return to make them all sorry. But Mr. Carpenter had given the little fat man such a shaking and thumping that everyone was sure he would not really come back.

So Toofie suggested to the Raggedys, "Let's visit the new families and see if they need any help."

Raggedy Andy thought this was a fine idea but asked, "Will it be all right if Raggedy Ann and I go along together and stop at the houses near the tree with the golden ring? And you can visit the houses on the other side."

Since Toofie was agreeable to this, off they all went. The Raggedys stopped first and knocked at the door of the Lizard family.

"Come in, come in," said Lena Lizard. She thanked them for their offer to help, but told them all their work was done. So the Raggedys left to go on to the Field Mouse house. Just as Raggedy Ann lifted her hand to knock at the front door, Raggedy Andy grabbed her arm and gasped, "Look, Raggedy Ann! Look at the tree with the golden rings!"

Raggedy Ann turned around, and then turned again, for she could not see the tree with golden rings hanging from it.

"Where, Raggedy Andy? I don't even see it!" she exclaimed.

"That's just it, Raggedy Ann. Don't you remember, it was right here between Toofie's house and the Field Mouse's home?" Raggedy Andy said.

"Could it have disappeared?" Raggedy Ann wondered as she walked around, looking at all the lovely green trees. But then she exclamied, "Oh no! Look here, Raggedy Andy!"

29

And she pointed to a brown, withered tree with one little golden ring hanging from a drooping branch.

Raggedy Andy ran over and he could hardly believe his eyes. What had been a beautiful green, leafy tree with golden rings sparkling all over its gay branches was now a brown, dried clump of drooping branches. And just one golden ring was left. It was as if the golden ring was a reminder of what the tree once had been.

The two little rag dolls were surprised and sad of course; immediately they wondered if the fat man, Dinkie, had done something to the tree.

Raggedy Andy suggested, "Let's see if we can find Dinkie and hear what he has to say about this."

But before they had gone very far, the Raggedys heard heavy footsteps chasing them. Turning around, they saw Dinkie coming along the path, huffing and puffing. He looked so mean and disagreeable that Raggedy Ann thought perhaps it would be helpful to have Toofie around.

"Oh Toofie," Raggedy Ann called, "here comes that disagreeable fat man who was here a while ago."

But Toofie was not in his house, or anywhere around. So the Raggedys ran toward the grocery store to get Mr. Carpenter's help.

But when Dinkie caught sight of the Raggedys, he ran so fast that he reached them before they could get to the grocery store and he bellowed, "I know just who is responsible for this town. It's you two! I shall take you down to the brook and tie you on a log and roll the log into the water. Then the brook will carry you down to the ocean and soon a boat will come along and hit the log. When it sinks to the bottom of the ocean, you will go with it."

And the little fat man carried the Raggedys down toward the brook and even though they both wiggled and twisted and squirmed as hard as they could.

"Now both of you sit there until I find a log," the fat man cried as he shoved the Raggedys into a little tight space between two big rocks and gave them a hard thump on their heads.

Raggedy Ann and Raggedy Andy looked at each other and smiled, for, being stuffed with nice clean white cotton, the thump did not hurt them a bit. However, they were not happy at being squeezed so tight that the only thing they could move was their

shoe-button eyes. And the fat man soon found a thick log and came back. He asked Raggedy Andy, "Have you any string?"

"No, I haven't," Raggedy Andy replied politely.

"I'll have to have string to tie you to this log," the fat little man fretted.

"Why not just put us on the log and we can hold on tight?" Raggedy Ann suggested, winking one shoe-button eye at her rag doll friend.

"Ha! You can't fool me that easily!" the fat man cried. "You would jump off the log as soon as it floated around the bend, I'm sure."

"Why don't you run up to Toofie's magic grocery store and get a piece of string?" Raggedy Andy asked.

"That's a good idea," Dinkie said. "I just saw the carpenter leave the grocery and walk away through the woods, so it will be safe for me to go there."

And off he ran to the grocery store.

When he was out of sight, Raggedy Andy asked, "How will we ever get out of this, Raggedy Ann?"

And before she could answer, they saw their friend, Mr. Carpenter coming through the woods. Quickly he rolled one of the heavy rocks away.

"Hurry, and hide behind this tree," the carpenter said as he rolled the stone back. "I followed Dinkie and saw him capture you, so I fooled him."

As the Raggedys and the carpenter were settled safely behind a huge tree, Dinkie came running up carrying a large bolt of string.

"Now I shall fix those Raggedys so that we shall never see them again," he said as he bent over to roll

the stone away and get the Raggedys.

But as he stooped over, the carpenter quietly tip-toed out and hit him with a barrel stave. It was such a hard crack that all the woodland creatures around thought a gun had been shot off! And Dinkie, too, thinking he had been shot, jumped over the log. *Splash!* He went right into the cold brook water. And while he scrambled up the other bank, the carpenter and the Raggedys hid.

"I'll run home and get some dry clothes," the fat man howled as he ran off, dripping wet.

The Raggedys and the carpenter had to hold their hands over their mouths to keep from laughing out loud. And off they went, merrily, to the grocery store, to have some refreshments. They had nine ice-cream cones each, they had become so hungry!

When they had finished, Raggedy Ann told Mr. Carpenter about the tree with the golden rings, and that they had forgotten to ask Dinkie if he had done something to the tree. And, as they sat wondering what to do, the door opened and in walked the little fat man once more.

CHAPTER 4

"AHA!" HE SHOUTED as he walked up to Raggedy
Ann. "I left you and Raggedy Andy down by the
brook squeezed in between two heavy stones. How
ever did you escape?"

"We didn't escape!" Raggedy Ann laughed. "The
nice kind-hearted carpenter rolled the heavy stone
away and set us free."

"I thought so," the little fat man howled. Now
he was indeed very angry with the carpenter, for not
only had the carpenter given Dinkie a hard smack
with a barrel stave and sent him flying into the brook,
but he had set the Raggedys free.

"This time," the little fat man screamed, "I will
get you Raggedys and I will get the carpenter too!"

But the carpenter did not seem to be one bit afraid
of Dinkie and answered him calmly, "I shall not let
you take the Raggedys."

And to their surprise, the Raggedys heard the voice
of Toofie who had quietly crept in while Dinkie was
screaming. "And I shall help Mr. Carpenter too."

"Oh, is that so?" the fat man howled. "Well, just wait until you see who I have to help me! I have brought three wild cougars to help me capture the Raggedys. And after that, I shall destroy the Tiny Town and all who are in it; then I will have the magic grocery store and everything else in it for myself."

"You say that you have brought three cougars to help you?" Toofie asked with a smile.

"Yes sir!" Dinkie answered. "Three of the wildest, fiercest cougars you would ever care to meet. They could tear you to pieces in almost a minute if they wanted to. I have to hold them back with all my strength to keep them from eating everyone."

Toofie smiled more widely as he asked, "Mister Fat Man, have these fierce wild cougars great big long teeth and very sharp claws?"

"That is just how they look, Toofie. And I would not act so pleased if I were you," replied Dinkie.

"Ha, ha, ha!" Toofie laughed as he felt the magic charms in his pocket. "Those are funny-looking cougars you have outside, Mr. Fat Man. I have never seen funnier ones in all my life."

"You'd better take another look, Mr. Toofie; I'll bet you will shake in your boots," howled Dinkie.

Toofie said, "We shall see," and he and the Raggedys and the fat man walked out the door. There sat three large, rubber cougars filled with air!

"Why," the fat man cried, "something has happened to my cougars!"

Toofie ran up to the first rubber cougar and kicked it hard. "Whoof," it went sailing up into the air.

Then he did the same thing to the other two cougars while the fat man looked on in surprise.

Then when Toofie started to run toward the fat man as if he would kick him too, Dinkie cried, "I won't stay here and be kicked about as you have kicked my cougars," and away he ran.

Then Toofie turned to the Raggedys and winked, saying, "Now watch!" for he still had his fingers on his magic charms in his pocket.

As he said this, the rubber cougars changed into real, live, fierce, wild cougars! They ran after the fat man howling, "We will teach you to bring us here where a magician changes us into rubber!"

Dinkie, afraid the cougars would catch him, was running faster than he ever had before. He was out of sight in a minute.

Raggedy Ann turned to see the carpenter coming out of the grocery store just then and she told him, "Well, you should have been here to see how Toofie changed the fierce wild cougars into rubber animals and kicked them clear across the road!"

The carpenter laughed. "I'll bet Dinkie was surprised and not very pleased."

Raggedy Andy said, "But he was even less pleased when Toofie changed them back into real live cougars and they started chasing him."

"I don't think we shall be bothered by the fat man any more today," said the carpenter as they all went into the store.

The Raggedys were perched up on a counter having a snack when Raggedy Ann happened to look out the door and saw the three wild cougars trying to hide behind a tree.

"Look," she said to her rag friend, "there are the three wild cougars and I'll bet they are hiding to catch some of the little woodland creatures as they leave the grocery store."

"Let's think of a way to trick them," said Raggedy Andy and he went to Toofie and told him about the cougars waiting outside.

Toofie put his hand in his pocket to get his magic charms and told Raggedy Andy, "Take a string of hot dogs out to the cougars, Raggedy Andy."

So, dragging behind him a long string of hot dogs, Raggedy Andy ran out the front door and across to the fierce cougars.

The first wild cougar sprang out and knocked Raggedy Andy down. "My, he smells wonderful!"

And the second cougar screamed, "Leave some of him for me!"

But the third cougar said, "Sillies, it isn't the rag doll—it's the string of meat that smells so good. Here let me have some!"

With that, they all jumped on the string of hot dogs and each grabbed a section.

As soon as the three cougars had sunk their teeth into the meat, Raggedy Andy jumped to his feet and hid behind a bush, for he knew something was going to happen to the animals. And sure enough, the string of hot dogs began to act very queerly. It swung this way and that, up and down, here and there. It shook the three cougars up against trees and stones.

My, how they howled and screamed! And they sounded even funnier because their teeth were sunk into the hot dogs. The harder the string of hot dogs shook, the more the cougars howled! But of course they could not let go, because of Toofie's magic. If Raggedy Andy had not known what was happening, he would have been quite frightened.

Finally the string of hot dogs pulled and tossed the cougars over to the ice-cold brook and in they went. They were doused up and down as though they were pieces of rags, and splashed every which way too. By this time, the cougars were very tired.

So the string of hot dogs pulled them up the bank of the brook and slammed them into the prickly bushes before shaking them loose.

The cougars were so exhausted that they could not run even after they had been freed but they went slinking away through the woods.

Raggedy Andy took the string of hot dogs and planted them in the earth near a tree. He knew that, because they were magical hot dogs, they would grow into a nice hot-dog bush so that anyone passing by would be able to pick them.

When he joined Raggedy Ann, who had been waiting in the grocery store, she told him, "That was a good trick to play on those cougars. Now maybe they will go far, far away and never come back."

Then, turning to Toofie, she said, "I think that Raggedy Andy and I will have to leave you now."

"Oh, please stay and live here with us in Tiny Town," Toofie pleaded. "Mr. Carpenter and I will

38

build you a little house, and we would so love to have you stay with us."

But Raggedy Ann with a happy smile answered, "Thank you so much, Toofie; it would be pleasant here, but Raggedy Andy and I must run along in search of more adventures."

"Ha!" a gruff voice boomed just then. "If you are looking for adventures, we shall be happy to provide some for you."

And before Toofie could get his hands on his magic charms, two of the cougars picked the Raggedys up with their teeth while the third pushed Toofie and the carpenter down on their faces.

And the three fierce cougars carried Raggedy Ann and Raggedy Andy to their home way back in a damp, musty corner of the woods, where the sunlight never shone. Their house was very dark too, with only one little window and one door.

"What shall we do with them?" growled one of the cougars after they had put the Raggedys down.

"Maybe we could make some beef stew out of them," answered his brother.

"Raggedy Ann and I are only rag dolls," Raggedy Andy told the cougars. "If you cook us, we would taste like dishwater and not like beef stew at all."

"He's just trying to fool us," said the third cougar as he brought a large kettle from the pantry and put it on the stove. "Now, as soon as the water boils, we will put them in the pot," he said. "And while I make the beef stew, you two can set the table."

He watched the pot until the water boiled.

"If you please, fierce, wild cougar," Raggedy Andy said to the cougar cook, "will you put me into the pot first?"

"Certainly," agreed the cougar cook. "I was going to do that anyway, because it was you who fooled us with the magic hot dogs."

So, as the other two cougars watched, he stuffed Raggedy Andy right into the large pot of boiling water. But before the cougars could jump back out of the way, Raggedy Andy splashed his arms and legs so hard that he splashed boiling water on the fierce animals. And, howling with pain and anger, they ran out the door and headed for the brook.

Raggedy Andy climbed out of the pot and, holding hands, he and Raggedy Ann ran outside, around the house, and into the bushes.

"They will not get any beef stew tonight." Raggedy Andy laughed. Then he added, "Whew, I got a nice hot bath!"

"You look very nice and clean." Raggedy Ann chuckled. "And I'm sure you will cool off quickly."

"Now, while the cougars are still at the brook, we had better run away from here as quickly as possible," Raggedy Andy suggested.

So the two rag dolls, joining hands, started to run. But to their surprise, they met an old friend, Grampy Hoppytoad, as he was sunning himself on a large rock.

"Well, Raggedy Ann and Raggedy Andy," Grampy Hoppytoad exclaimed as he hopped out into the path. "Why are you running so fast?"

41

The Raggedys sat down on an old stump to explain. "We are running away from three wild, fierce cougars. Would you happen to know them, Grampy?"

"Yes, indeed!" Gampy Hoppytoad answered as he lit his pipe of mullein leaves. "They are Charlie, Karlie and Kenneth Cougar. They are the fiercest cougars for miles around."

"That's what they told us, Grampy Hoppytoad," Raggedy Ann said. "They wanted to make beef stew out of Raggedy Andy and me but Raggedy Andy splashed boiling water over them and you should have seen them run!"

"Hmm!" Grampy Hoppytoad mused. "I imagine that will make them very angry."

"Yes," Raggedy Andy said. "But we did not want to be made into beef stew or anything else for that matter!"

"Of course not." Grampy Hoppytoad laughed as he puffed his pipe. "Besides, they can't make beef stew out of rag dolls!"

Just then a loud howl echoed from deep within the woods. Then there was another howl which sounded closer, and finally there was a third howl which was the loudest and closest of all.

"Goodness," Raggedy Ann exclaimed, "it must be Charlie, Karlie and Kenneth again! Don't they make a lot of noise?"

"We must hide," Grampy Hoppytoad said. "The fierce, wild cougars can run very fast and they will be right here in a moment."

CHAPTER 5

GRAMPY HOPPYTOAD quickly hid in a large hollow log lying on the ground near by and pulled the Raggedys in beside him.

"The three fierce cougars will not think of looking for us in here," Grampy Hoppytoad whispered.

Peeping through a knot hole in the log, he could see the cougars coming and he told the Raggedys, "Here they are! We must be very still."

The three fierce, wild cougars came running near the log, all of them howling as loudly as they could.

"Ha!" Charlie screeched as he sniffed all around. "They are near us; I can smell them!"

"Ahaaaaa!" Karlie and Kenneth howled together, "they must be inside that log!"

"Shall I run home for an ax and cut the log in two?" Kenneth asked.

"Yes," Karlie and Charlie replied. "We shall stay and watch the log to make sure they do not escape."

So Kenneth ran home after the ax, howling all the way. Charlie and Karlie sat down on the log to keep watch. All was quiet in the woods. Then Grampy Hoppytoad noticed the tip of Charlie Cougar's tail curling around inside the log.

"Ha!" Grampy whispered to the Raggedys. "Let's catch hold of his tail and tie it around this stick I have fastened here. When he jumps up, he will pull his tail into a hard knot and he will not be able to get free."

Raggedy Andy did this so slowly and carefully with his soft cotton hands that Charlie did not even feel it.

Then Grampy Hoppytoad put his mouth to the knot hole and groaned, *"Booooo, Booooooo!"*

Karlie Cougar said, "It sounds as if there is a Boogar inside this log," and he stooped down and put his eye to the knot hole.

Inside, Grampy Hoppytoad was ready with a huge mouthful of smoke from his pipe which he blew right into Karlie's eye. Karlie jumped six feet into the air, yelped and turned around to run for home as fast as he could.

Charlie, not knowing what had happened, laugh-

ingly remarked, "Hm, I guess he is going home to help Kenneth find the ax."

Then Grampy Hoppytoad pinched Charlie's tail very hard, and this time is was Charlie's turn to jump into the air, but he could not jump very far because his tail was tied to the stick. And while he howled and clawed and scratched with anger, the Raggedys and Grampy Hoppytoad scampered out of the log and escaped into the bushes.

The two rag dolls and their friend had had such exciting adventures that they were quite tired by this time. And they were hungry and thirsty too.

Grampy Hoppytoad suggested, "Let's hunt around and see if we can find a soda-water spring."

So the Raggedys and Grampy Hoppytoad hunted all around in the deep, deep woods for a soda-water spring, but they could find none. However, they did find a root-beer tree with a faucet set into it. Right beneath the faucet was a stand with a stack of pretty pink cups. After Raggedy Ann and Raggedy Andy and Grampy Hoppytoad each had nine glasses of the cold, foamy root beer, they set out in search of a patch of cream puffs, or some doughnuts.

Although they searched for a long time, they could not find a single doughnut field or patch of cream puffs. Finally, after crossing the brook, they found something to eat.

As they came to a small clearing, Raggedy Andy, who was leading the little group, tossed his cap into the air and kicked up his heels, crying, "Whoopee! Come see what I have found!"

Grampy Hoppytoad and Raggedy Ann came running as fast as they could to find a patch of the tastiest looking pies they had ever seen.

"Now we shall have a feast!" Grampy Hoppytoad said as he picked a tasty pie.

"I should say we will have a nice feast!" a loud gruff voice growled, and out of the bushes came the three fierce, wild cougars.

"We are hungry!" Charlie Cougar howled louder than ever.

"We want beef stew!" the other two cougars howled.

"Well," Grampy Hoppytoad said, "neither of the Raggedys have any beef stew in their pockets, but if you would like a pie, you may have this."

He handed Charlie Cougar a pie. Then he picked two more and handed one each to Karlie and Kenneth.

"We are very, very hungry," the three cougars cried. "We had to work very hard to get Charlie's tail untied after you played that trick on us."

Then, as they started to gobble the pies, a strange look came over all three faces, and they broke out into terrible yelps and screams.

"Ouch, my mouth burns!" howled Kenneth as all three cougars danced up and down, kicking.

"I guess these must be April Fool pies," Grampy Hoppytoad whispered. "Let's escape while they take care of their tummy aches."

So the Raggedys took Grampy Hoppytoad's hands and ran with him until they came to a patch of lovely

cream puffs. But these were not filled with red pepper as the pies had been, so the three friends had a very pleasant little picnic all by themselves.

"It was lucky that you thought to give the cougars those pies, Grampy!" Raggedy Ann said. "How did you know that they were April Fool pies?"

"I didn't know it." Grampy Hoppytoad laughed. "I just thought if I could feed them enough pies, the cougars would not be very hungry and would not want to make beef stew out of you."

"I am sorry the pies burned them so," Raggedy Ann said, "for although the cougars have been very unpleasant, I do not want to see anyone feel sick."

"Neither do I, Raggedy Ann," said Grampy Hoppytoad.

Raggedy Ann, Raggedy Andy and Grampy Hoppytoad walked along through the pleasant woods until they came to another pie patch. This was much larger than the other and the pies looked better too.

"I do not think we should eat these, Raggedys," Grampy Hoppytoad said. "They may be April Fool pies too."

47

"I know what to do," Raggedy Andy said. "I shall taste one of the pies, for red pepper does not burn me. Then, if the pies are real ones, I shall be able to tell you."

So Raggedy Andy picked a lemon meringue pie. When he tasted it, he found it was delicious, so he gave it to Raggedy Ann. Then he picked a strawberry pie and gave it to nice old Grampy Hoppytoad. When he had picked a chocolate cream pie for himself, he sat down beside his friends and ate every bit of it.

Just then, the three fierce, wild cougars came dashing out of the bushes howling very loudly, "Now we have you and we shall take you home and make beef stew out of you!"

Raggedy Ann said very politely, "Please, Charlie, Karlie and Kenneth, wouldn't you rather have something truly good?"

"Beef stew is very, very good!" the three cougars howled again.

"Oh yes, indeed," Raggedy Ann agreed, "but really and truly, you cannot make beef stew out of Raggedy Andy and me, for we are only rag dolls and stuffed with cotton. You just taste one of these pies instead. Then you will not even want any beef stew."

"Yes, and have the pies burn our mouths!" Charlie Cougar coughed.

But when Raggedy Ann showed them the pies had no red hot pepper in them, the three fierce cougars each took a bite of a wonderful apple pie.

"Gracious!" Charlie exclaimed.

His brothers agreed. "Goodness!" they said.

And, just as Raggedy Ann had promised, they discovered that the pies were very tasty. Raggedy Andy suggested, "Let's all have a pie picnic!"

And so they did. Charlie and Karlie and Kenneth enjoyed the pies so much, they forgot to be fierce and wild. Instead they laughed and talked with the Raggedys and Grampy Hoppytoad as if they had all been the best of friends for years.

"Let's build a nice cougar home right near the pie patch," Charlie said, as Raggedy Ann, Raggedy Andy and Grampy Hoppytoad finally got up to go.

Raggedy Ann smiled and said, "If you three cougar boys live here very long, you will soon be three pleasant, tame cougars."

But the three cougar brothers laughed and said, "I don't know how that could happen."

Grampy Hoppytoad, who was older than the Raggedys, suddenly said, "I think I will have to rest a bit before we go on. I'll just have a short nap and then we'll be ready."

So while the three cougars busied themselves eating one pie after another, Grampy Hoppytoad and the Raggedys sat down. The Raggedys smiled at Grampy's loud, long snores.

Suddenly Charlie Cougar sighed and said, "After eating sixteen pies apiece, my brothers and I think maybe we are not so fierce and wild as we used to be. So we want you to tell us: What do we have to do to become friendly, tame cougars, Raggedy Ann?"

The sweet rag doll laughed and answered, "It will really be quite easy, because it is much more fun being nice and kind than it is being fierce and cruel! All you have to do is this: When you meet anyone, just stop and think, 'How can I show this person that I am a friend?' A little teeny voice inside you will tell you just how you can do it."

"Must we stop howling too?" Karlie asked. "I have never liked to hear Charlie and Kenneth howl, but I enjoyed doing it myself."

"Probably they did not like to hear you either." Raggedy Ann laughed.

"That is quite true," Charlie and Kenneth said.

"Then we must all stop howling," Karlie Cougar decided.

"Why don't you build a cozy little house near the pie patch?" Raggedy Andy asked.

But before they could think about this, Raggedy Ann said, "I have a better idea. I could run back to Toofie's nice Tiny Town and ask Toofie and Mr. Carpenter to build you a nice cozy Cougar house there. For if you are friendly and tame, Toofie will be glad to have you live there. And you can have everything you wish at his magic store free of charge."

"Whee!" the three, nice tame cougars cried. "Let's run back and ask Toofie!"

After shaking hands with the Raggedys and Grampy Hoppytoad, the three happy Cougars, Charlie, Karlie and Kenneth ran gaily back through the woods without howling once.

CHAPTER 6

As the Raggedys and Grampy Hoppytoad skipped gaily through the woods, they chatted about the cougars.

Grampy Hoppytoad asked, "How ever did you happen to meet them?"

So Raggedy Andy told Grampy all about the little fat man who had brought the cougars to capture the Raggedys.

Raggedy Ann clapped her hands to her mouth and exclaimed, "Goodness gracious me! I forgot all about why we were searching for the little fat man. Don't you remember, Raggedy Andy? We wanted to ask him what he knew about the tree with the golden ring?"

Raggedy Andy thought for a moment. "Perhaps if we look around, we might still be able to find him."

Grampy Hoppytoad heaved a big sigh and said, "This might be exciting, but I am afraid you will have to go on without me. I am all out of breath and I must stop to rest."

"Oh, we shall be very glad to wait for you, Grampy Hoppytoad," offered Raggedy Ann. "Let's all sit here near this lovely clear brook and have a rest. When we are refreshed, we shall look for Dinkie."

And as they sat on the bank of the brook, a strange little creature wearing pointed shoes and a pointed cap ran up and stood directly in front of Grampy Hoppytoad.

In a high, squeaky voice, he demanded, "Do you know where I can find Raggedy Ann?"

Grampy wiggled and waggled his large eyes this way and that to keep from laughing.

"If Raggedy Ann were a snake, she would bite you, she is so close." Grampy chuckled.

"No, I wouldn't, Grampy Hoppytoad!" Raggedy Ann laughed.

Without a word, the strange little creature grabbed Raggedy Ann, and before Raggedy Andy could help, he had dashed off with her into the bushes. Of course, as soon as Raggedy Andy and Grampy could get to their feet, they followed. But they could not run half so fast as the creature, who seemed to disappear before their eyes. They looked this way and that, but could see neither Raggedy Ann nor the creature. But they kept looking and, in a few minutes, what they did see was a little line of crumbs.

Now Raggedy Ann, knowing that her rag doll friend and Grampy Hoppytoad would never be able to keep up with this fast creature, wondered how they could find her. Suddenly she remembered the piece of pie she had put in her pocket when they were all at the pie patch. Reaching into her pocket, she found a handful of crumbs. Quickly she began scattering them behind her.

And this was the line of crumbs Raggedy Andy and Grampy Hoppytoad found. They followed it until they came to a strange eight-sided house. Above the front door was a sign which read, "Gilly Imp, Mischief Maker."

Grampy Hoppytoad put on his spectacles and read the sign.

"Dear me!" he exclaimed as he wiped his forehead with his blue pocket hankie and sat down on a rock.

"Why do you say 'Dear Me!' Grampy?" Raggedy Andy asked.

"Because," Grampy replied, "Gilly Imp is known to be a mean little creature who can work magic. And besides, he is very selfish and unkind to others. There is no telling what he will do to Raggedy Ann."

At this, Gilly Imp put his head out of a window and cried, "You will never see Raggedy Ann again, because I have heard that she has a candy heart and I need it. So I will snip her open and take it!"

Slam! went the window and Raggedy Andy and Grampy Hoppytoad were left below wondering what to do. After they had thought and thought for a long time, Grampy Hoppytoad had an idea.

He said, "I will go around to the back and crawl under the house and light my pipe. Then I will blow the smoke up through the floor. If Gilly Imp runs out of the house, then you can run in and rescue Raggedy Ann."

So that was just what they did.

As soon as Gilly Imp saw the smoke coming up through his floor, he yelled, "Fire, Fire!" and ran out of the house carrying a bucket.

While he raced to the brook for water, Raggedy Andy rushed into the house and found Raggedy Ann who was tied to a chair. He quickly loosened the rope and together they rushed out to find Grampy Hoppytoad who was waiting at the door.

They ran and ran without a stop until at last they came to a lovely lollypop field beside a soda-water spring. Then of course they stopped, for the lolly-pops and soda-water looked very good. And they soon forgot all about Gilly Imp, the Mischief Maker.

Meanwhile, Gilly Imp, the Mischief Maker, ran to the brook for a pail of water, crying, "My house is on fire! My house is on fire!" all the way there and all the way back home.

Next door to Gilly Imp lived a Bugaboo. The Bugaboo was a strange little fellow too, who was very selfish and unkind.

When he heard Gilly Imp cry "Fire!" the Bugaboo

ran out of his house and followed Gilly, crying, "Hurrah! Gilly Imp's house is on fire. Hurrah!"

When they returned to Gilly's house, however, they could not find any fire. The smoke which Grampy Hoppytoad had blown up through the floor had completely disappeared.

"I don't see any fire," the Bugaboo said.

"The smoke is gone," Gilly Imp replied. "And Raggedy Ann is gone too! I had her tied to this chair because I wanted to take her candy heart out of her."

"Ha, ha, ha!" The Bugaboo laughed meanly. "I didn't know that you had captured Raggedy Ann. I could have told you what happened to her when you ran to the brook."

"What could you have told me, Bugaboo?" Gilly Imp inquired.

"Why," the Bugaboo said, "after you ran out of your house yelling, 'Fire,' I saw Raggedy Andy and Raggedy Ann running out of your house. Then I saw Grampy Hoppytoad come crawling out from under your house with his pipe in his mouth."

"Aha! I see it all now," Gilly Imp cried. "Grampy Hoppytoad blew the smoke up through the floor of my house, just as I was about to snip open Raggedy Ann to get her candy heart."

"Is the candy heart wonderful?" the Bugaboo asked.

"Oh dear me, yes!" Gilly Imp replied. "It must be a magic candy heart because everyone loves Raggedy Ann. That is why I want it; then everyone will love me."

55

"I need one too," the Bugaboo said, "because no one loves me either."

"Then we shall follow the Raggedys and Grampy Hoppytoad and get the candy hearts. I shall take Raggedy Ann's and you may take Raggedy Andy's," said Gilly Imp.

Raggedy Andy did not have a candy heart, but Gilly Imp and the Bugaboo did not know this. So they ran after the Raggedys and presently they came to the lollypop field where the Raggedys and Grampy Hoppytoad were eating lollypops and drinking ice-cream sodas.

"We want your candy hearts!" Gilly Imp cried, catching Raggedy Ann.

"We want your candy hearts!" the Bugaboo cried, catching Raggedy Andy.

"Did Gilly Imp tell you I had a candy heart?" Raggedy Andy whispered as the Bugaboo began running with him.

"Yes," the Bugaboo told him.

"Then he told a fib to fool you." Raggedy Andy laughed. "Only Raggedy Ann has a candy heart."

Not believing this, the Bugaboo carefully felt all over Raggedy Andy's shirt, but of course he could not feel any candy heart. He dropped Raggedy Andy right there and ran after Gilly Imp.

"You told me that Raggedy Andy has a candy heart!" the Bugaboo said angrily, as he caught hold of Gilly Imp.

Just then Raggedy Andy caught up with them, picked up a stick and he hit Gilly Imp with it.

"Ouch!" cried Gilly, dropping Raggedy Ann and punching the Bugaboo.

Then the Bugaboo punched Gilly Imp. So they wrestled and tussled and pushed and punched each other until they both stumbled and went rolling down the bank into the brook.

By the time they scrambled out of the brook, climbed up the bank and shook themselves, they could not find the Raggedys or Grampy Hoppytoad.

Of course, Grampy and his rag doll friends had scampered away through the woods. By the time Gilly Imp and the Bugaboo ran home to change their clothes, the three friends were far, far, away, laughing at the way they had fooled Gilly Imp, the Mischief Maker, and his friend, the Bugaboo.

"I know where we can have lots of fun, and it isn't very far from here either," Grampy Hoppytoad said.

"If you are not too tired to go further, then let us go there right now, Grampy," said Raggedy Ann.

So they crawled under some bushes and found another path which they followed for a long way. But suddenly Grampy Hoppytoad stopped, scratched his head, and looked all about. "I am afraid we are on the wrong path," he exclaimed.

Just then they heard a voice crying, "Oh, dear, oh dear!" So they ran to see what the trouble was. They followed a bend in the road and they came to a big, huge, tremendous giant. Although the giant was sitting on a large hill, he was still so much taller than they that they could hardly see his face. But they could hear his loud sobs. And at his feet was a pool of water which came from the tears rolling off his cheeks.

Even though he was so tremendous, the giant looked and sounded just like a little boy who had dropped his lollypop on the ground. So the Raggedys and Grampy Hoppytoad were not a bit frightened.

"Why do you sit there crying so loudly, Mr. Giant?" Raggedy Ann asked as she climbed a tree to get closer to him.

"Because," the giant sobbed, "I stepped on a bee and it stung the heel of my foot!"

"Let me get the sting out," suggested Raggedy Andy kindly. "Then it will feel much better."

While Raggedy Andy was taking care of the giant's foot, Raggedy Ann asked, "Where were you going, Mr. Giant?"

The giant told her, "I was on my way to the grocery store to get some food so I could make dinner for all the little boys and girls who live with me. They do not have any mothers or fathers, so I take care of them, and we have lots of fun together."

"I am glad to hear that you are a kind-hearted giant," exclaimed Raggedy Ann. "Some children and even some grownups think that giants are mean to little children."

"I just wish I could find the person who started telling such stories," blustered the giant in his loud voice. "I would show that person that giants are just as nice as small people, and they have much bigger hearts."

Raggedy Andy had removed the sting by this time, and the giant thanked him very nicely. So Raggedy Ann climbed down from the tree and the Raggedys were saying good-by to the giant, when along came the Bugaboo and Gilly Imp.

Without a word, they each caught hold of one of Raggedy Ann's arms. One pulled one way, and one pulled the other until Raggedy Ann could feel the stitches in her dress start to rip.

"Stop," she cried. "Let go of me!"

"We want your candy heart," the two mischievous creatures screamed.

Raggedy Andy pushed Gilly Imp and then grabbed the Bugaboo. But they both turned and were ready to fight the little rag doll.

59

Just then the giant bent down and, as easy as pie, picked up Gilly Imp in one hand and the Bugaboo in the other. And before they could open their mouths to yell, he had bumped their heads together so hard they saw stars!

"Now I think you will leave my friends alone," he said.

"Please let them go, Mr. Giant," said Raggedy Ann.

So the giant put the two little mean creatures down on the ground and gave them each a gentle smack. They were so happy to be out of the giant's hands that they scooted away while the Raggedys laughed.

"Now," said the giant, "perhaps you had better come along with me until those creatures are too far away to bother you again."

"That would be fun," agreed Grampy Hoppytoad.

So the giant picked up the rag dolls and Grampy Hoppytoad and carefully put them in the brim of his hat. It was great fun to get such a nice ride.

"This is almost like being in an airplane," giggled Raggedy Ann.

The giant's hat brim was so large that the three friends were able to walk around from one side to another, and even have a game of tag.

When they came to the grocery store in a part of the woods they had never seen before, they found that the grocery store keeper was a giant too. He had a very jolly face and twinkling eyes, and gave them some cookies to eat while they waited for the kindly giant to shop.

When he had gathered all his things, the kindly giant put all the food in a giant basket which he carried easily. And off they went to the giant's house to see all the children.

But just as they came to a bend in the road, the giant tripped. Down he went, flying through the air, his great basket crashing to the ground. And of course, his hat flew off his head, so the Raggedys and Grampy went sailing through the air.

Although the tumble did not hurt Raggedy Ann one bit, as soon as she hit the ground, she was grabbed by Gilly Imp. For it was he who had stretched a wire across the ground to trip the giant.

The giant sat up just in time to see Gilly Imp running off through the woods with Raggedy Ann. And the Bugaboo could be seen close behind him. When Raggedy Andy explained to the giant what had happened, the kindly giant spluttered, "We shall go to Gilly Imp's house and rescue Raggedy Ann this minute!"

And of course, the giant's legs were so long that, with only a few steps, he was right in front of the

Imp's little house. The doors and windows were locked tightly and not a sound was coming from within. Raggedy Andy politely knocked at the door, but no one answered.

"Ho, ho." The giant laughed. "If they want to play games, that's what we shall do."

He took out a pocket knife and quickly sliced the roof off the house, just as smoothly as you might cut a piece of cheese! He reached down inside, picked up Gilly Imp and the Bugaboo and tossed them into the brook. Then he gently picked up Raggedy Ann and placed her in the hat brim along with her friends.

"The next time I find those creatures bothering you, I shall snap off their heads," he exclaimed, winking his eye. But the creatures, hiding behind the house did not see his eye wink and they shivered.

Gilly Imp's teeth chattered as he said, "I shall never again bother the Raggedys."

And the Bugaboo agreed, "It's too dangerous!"

When the giant came to the place where all his groceries had spilled, the Raggedys and Grampy Hoppytoad got down to help him put everything back into the basket. And then they all went on to the giant's great big beautiful house, which stood on a hill.

At the sound of the kindly giant's "Hello," many, many children came out of the front door, and the back door, and even the side doors. They all gathered about the giant who picked up a handful gently and gave them all a very gentle hug.

Then there was much running to and fro while they opened all the bags and packages to see what the giant had brought. Soon all the children were chewing and munching all the delicious food.

The Raggedys and Grampy Hoppytoad had not realized they were hungry until they saw all the goodies, but then they ate too.

Suddenly Raggedy Ann saw something move in the bushes near-by and she whispered to Grampy, "I think I just saw Gilly Imp and the Bugaboo there. Do you think they have come to capture us again?"

Before Grampy could answer her, the two mean little creatures had crept out of the bushes pleading, "Please, Mr. Giant, we will not try to harm the Raggedys again; do not snap off our heads!"

The kindly giant said, very sternly, "How do I know you are telling the truth?"

Gilly Imp thought a moment and then admitted, "I know we have not acted very nicely, but we truly would like to be friends now. And, if you let us, we shall show you that we can keep our promises."

Raggedy Ann asked the giant, "Don't you think we could give them one last chance?"

So the giant agreed.

Gilly Imp and the Bugaboo were very happy and the Bugaboo suggested, "If you come with us, we will show you the nicest ice-cream mud puddle you ever did see."

The kindly giant said he could not leave his children then, so he told the Raggedys to call loudly if the creatures did not behave. And Raggedy Ann, Raggedy Andy, Grampy Hoppytoad, Gilly Imp and the Bugaboo went off together.

CHAPTER 7

GILLY IMP led the way across the brook and through the woods to a clearing and there in the center, was the ice-cream mud puddle. Only it wasn't mud at all—it was yellow, pink, and brown ice cream. The pink ice cream had cherries and strawberries in it, and the brown was chocolate, with bits of nuts sprinkled through it. And the yellow, of course, was lemon ice cream.

Raggedy Ann and Raggedy Andy and Grampy Hoppytoad were very glad that Gilly Imp and the Bugaboo wanted to be friends. And they decided that the two creatures had really changed and were as nice as could be.

Gilly Imp was just swallowing a huge mouthful of pink ice cream with strawberries and cherries, when he began to choke. After the Bugaboo had smacked him hard on the back, Gilly Imp was able to catch his breath.

Raggedy Ann inquired, "What happened? Are you all right now?"

Gilly Imp's mischievous eyes twinkled as he shouted happily, "I have just made a great discovery!"

Everyone was puzzled and looked around for something unusual.

But Gilly laughed as he explained, "No, no, it is nothing that you can see. But I have just seen something. Bugaboo, we do not need candy hearts to have friends. We only need to be nice to others and they will be our friends."

"Why, of course," exclaimed Raggedy Ann and Raggedy Andy together. "Didn't you know that?"

"No one ever told us," the little creatures said sadly. And Gilly Imp added, "But now that we have learned it, we shall never, never forget it."

At that moment, a loud, angry voice interrupted, "Someone has been eating from my ice-cream mud puddle!"

Raggedy Ann looked at Raggedy Andy, and said, "That sounds like the voice of Dinkie, the little fat man."

Raggedy Andy whispered, "Perhaps now we can find out what happened to the tree with the golden rings."

Now the Raggedys wanted to find Dinkie, so they did not get up and run. Besides, they had eaten so much ice cream that their little tummies were all filled and they could not possibly run. Sure enough, coming toward them was Dinkie, the little fat man, carrying a long stick.

"Someone has been eating from my ice-cream mud

puddle!" he shouted as he walked toward them. "And it is you Raggedys, just as I thought!"

With this, he gave Raggedy Andy a hard thump with the long stick.

Gilly Imp jumped up and said sharply, "See here, Raggedy Andy is my friend, and I will not let you hurt him."

Dinkie turned and, laughing hard, tried to smack Gilly with the stick too. But Gilly jumped back and out of the way. Then the little fat man tried to thump the Bugaboo with his long stick, but the Bugaboo jumped out of the way. Dinkie, angrier than ever, hit Raggedy Andy again.

"Ha, ha, ha!" Raggedy Andy laughed, doing a somersault backwards. "That didn't hurt my cotton stuffing a bit!"

But then Dinkie hit Raggedy Andy so hard that it made the stitches rip right out of Raggedy Andy's head and some of the cotton stuck out!

"Now then, Mister Dinkie, see what you have done," Raggedy Ann cried. "Aren't you ashamed of yourself?"

"Is that cotton sticking out of Raggedy Andy's head, truly?" the little fat man asked.

"Yes, it is," Raggedy Ann replied. "And you will have to take him home and sew him up."

"Aha!" Dinkie laughed. "I shall take him home all right, but I shall take all the cotton out of Raggedy Andy and use it for the mattress I am making for my bed."

Picking Raggedy Andy up, he started running with

WORTH GRUELLE

the rag doll who could not squirm out of Dinkie's hands. Raggedy Ann, Gilly Imp and the Bugaboo ran after Dinkie, but Grampy Hoppytoad was so tired by this time that he just hobbled after and could not catch up with them.

Dinkie kept ahead of the three friends although they ran quickly. He ran into his house and slammed the door behind him just as Raggedy Ann and her friends got there.

"Run and climb in the windows," shouted Raggedy Ann, but Dinkie locked the windows tightly before they could climb in.

Raggedy Ann called Gilly Imp and the Bugaboo aside and whispered, "I have an idea."

Soon the three took a wheelbarrow and three shovels which Raggedy Ann had seen propped up against the side of the house. And they went down to the ice-cream mud puddle.

When they returned to the house, the wheelbarrow was piled high with ice cream, which they heaped high all around the little man's house.

Soon they could hear him cry, "Oh, it is terribly cold in here. Whatever have you done?" And his teeth chattered like two hickory nuts.

"We shall make it even colder, if you do not let Raggedy Andy out," the Bugaboo shouted.

So Dinkie opened his door and came out with the rag doll, whose happy smile was still on his face. The Bugaboo grabbed Dinkie and washed his face in the ice cream. Dinkie did not like this one bit.

"Now you will sew up Raggedy Andy," Gilly Imp

cried. And Dinkie did so, silently and sullenly.

Then the little fat man, cold, wet and angry, turned and entered his little house.

But he shouted as soon as the door was locked, "Just you wait. After I have changed into dry, clean clothes, I will be back to deal with you."

When the Raggedys, laughing at how silly Dinkie had looked, got up to go, they found a surprise at the path near Dinkie's house. A tree had sprung up with beautiful golden rings shining all over its boughs.

Gilly Imp pointed to it in amazement, and the Bugaboo gasped, "My, how pretty! But where did it come from?"

So the Raggedys explained once more, as they had done for Toofie and the carpenter, that the tree was a magic sign. It meant that the fairies knew the little creatures were truly good and had done a kind deed when they rescued Raggedy Andy. Then they told Gilly Imp and the Bugaboo to shake the tree for their golden rings. When the two little creatures did so, two golden, glimmering circlets dropped at their feet.

Happily, they put the rings on their fingers and were starting off through the woods to find Grampy Hoppytoad when suddenly they heard a soft sob. It was the sound of someone crying.

"Let's find that unhappy sounding person first and see if we can help. Then we shall get Grampy Hoppytoad. He must be taking a nap at the ice-cream mud puddle."

But, glancing backward at the tree, they saw Dinkie, who had heard all about the tree and the rings as he changed his clothes. Dinkie was shaking the tree as hard as he could. But of course, no rings fell down for him.

He was so angry that he screamed, "I want a golden ring for good luck! It's not fair that I can't have any. It's not fair, not fair!"

But the Raggedys and their friends just ran off, laughing. Dinkie did look ridiculous.

Soon they came to a little boy sitting on a large rock. And the little boy was crying softly to himself. Raggedy Ann asked him what was wrong.

"I can't find my mama any place," the boy said.

"My." Raggedy Ann wiped the tears from his big brown eyes. "We shall take you home and see if we can find your mama. Come along."

So the little boy pointed out the road which led to his house, but when they got there, it was empty.

Raggedy Andy whispered to Raggedy Ann, "When we came into the garden, I saw an ice-cream cone bush, so I shall pick some ice-cream cones for all of us. Then maybe we can find out what has happened to the little boy's mother and daddy."

And sure enough, after the little boy had eaten three ice-cream cones—chocolate, strawberry, and maple—he was able to explain what had happened.

"My name is Ted," he told them. "And I like to walk in the woods, for the little animals are my friends. Well, this morning my daddy went out to chop some wood and I went for a walk. When I came back, my mama was not here. So I went out to search for her and my daddy. But I could not find them anywhere. I was going to look again when you came along. Will you help me?"

Just then there was a tap at the door, and Raggedy Ann ran to open it. To her surprise, she found Grampy Hoppytoad peering up at her. Grampy had awakened to hear the Raggedys scampering through the woods and, refreshed, he was able to follow them.

Now he said quite calmly, "I shall help you find Ted's mama and daddy. For I have magic green spectacles here, and I can see almost anyone."

So everyone watched as Grampy put on his spectacles and peered about. Slowly he left the little cottage, with Raggedy Ann, little Ted, Raggedy Andy, Gilly Imp and the Bugaboo walking behind him.

They had been walking only a few minutes when Gilly Imp exclaimed, "Why, we are going back along the road to Dinkie's house!"

But the Bugaboo, peering ahead, said, "No, I think we shall go right past it. I wonder if Dinkie knows where Ted's mama and daddy could be."

Of course the little band of friends could not know how nearly they had guessed the truth. They only kept walking and wondering. Grampy carefully followed the footsteps which led down a path, across another brook and into a deeper part of the lovely woods. In a short time they came to a darling little cottage and above the door was a sign which read, "Mrs. Merrie Witchie."

"Ha!" Grampy Hoppytoad exclaimed. "Maybe if we ask Mrs. Merrie Witchie, she can tell us how to find little Ted's nice mama and daddy."

"But Mrs. Merrie Witchie may be a very cross, peevish person in spite of her name. She may not help us at all," Raggedy Andy said.

A tiny window in the front door opened just then, and a sweet little woman put her head out.

She smiled pleasantly as she said, "Good day."

Raggedy Ann knew instantly that they had nothing to fear from such a friendly little woman. So she told Mrs. Merrie Witchie they were searching for little Ted's mama and daddy.

"Oh, dear!" the little woman exclaimed. "I shall have to use my magic charms. Wait a moment."

After she had joined them outside, she placed her magical charms on the ground and did a little dance around them. Raggedy Ann knew that they were very good charms, for there was a bit of pink ribbon, a piece of pretty lace, the picture of a baby, and a lovely blue hankie. After a while, Mrs. Merrie Witchie sat down and seemed to be thinking hard.

"Do you know," she said, "little Ted's mama and

daddy did pass by here early today, but they were being carried away by some sort of magic. It will take you a while to find them, so you had better come in and have something to eat first."

So the Raggedys and all their friends went into the little cottage where Mrs. Merrie Witchie gave them a very, very nice lunch.

When they had finished with some chocolate cookies and ice cream, she said, "I believe the best way for you to travel will be with some magic scooters which I shall make for you now."

So she got out her magic charms again and made three magic scooters.

Just as they were ready to start, Mrs. Merrie Witchie told them, "All you have to do is stand on these scooters and they will carry you along wherever you want to go."

So off they went—Raggedy Ann in front with little Ted, Raggedy Andy behind with Grampy Hoppytoad and last of all came Gilly Imp and the Bugaboo.

What they did not know was that behind all of them, following closely and silently was Dinkie.

CHAPTER 8

THE RAGGEDYS and their friends rode on their magic scooters, gliding away down the path through the lovely whispering woods. When they came to a tree which had fallen across the path, instead of having to get off and lift the scooters over the fallen tree, they raised the front wheel ever so lightly. Then, *whoosh,* they sailed over the tree without a single bump or jar! It was lots of fun and they almost wished that there were more fallen trees.

Raggedy Andy had brought along a basket in which Mrs. Merrie Witchie had packed a lunch. So, when they grew hungry after following the footprints for a long, long time, they rested the scooters against trees. Then they sat down for a nice picnic lunch. They had hardly started eating when Dinkie came hopping along the path and ran right up to them.

"Why are you sitting here eating your lunch?" he asked in an angry tone.

He was hot and tired because he had had to run very fast to keep up with the magic scooters.

"Because we are hungry," Raggedy Andy replied. "And besides, where did you come from?"

"I have been following you all the time," Dinkie said sulkily. Then he added, "Ow, my feet hurt so!"

"Sit down and rest," said Raggedy Ann kindly. She smiled at Dinkie, hoping it would make him friendly. "You may have something to eat too."

But as Raggedy Ann held out a cream puff, Dinkie snapped it from her hand and threw it against the tree where it smashed into pieces.

"What a mean, rude person!" Raggedy Andy cried. "Let's not pay any attention to him."

"Maybe you do not know who I am!" the little fat man shouted in a loud voice.

"Oh, maybe we do not wish to know!" Raggedy Andy thought to himself, but did not say it. "Why don't you tell us then?" he suggested instead.

The little fat man almost burst with pride as he spluttered, "I am the Magician's Messenger and I am here to see that you do not find little Ted's mama and daddy. For the Magician has taken them to his castle to work for him."

Little Ted, hearing this, burst into sobs and tears. But Raggedy Ann was able to comfort him.

She put her soft cotton-stuffed arms around little Ted and whispered, "Do not mind Dinkie! I am very, very sure we shall find your mama and daddy. Trust us and you will see."

So little Ted stopped his crying, put his arms around Raggedy Ann and kissed her lovingly.

But before they knew what was happening, Dinkie

scampered along the path, dived into the bushes ahead, and then disappeared before their eyes.

The Raggedys and all their friends quickly hopped onto their magic scooters and followed Dinkie.

"I think we are getting closer and closer to the Magician's place," Raggedy Ann said after a while.

"What makes you think that?" asked Grampy Hoppytoad.

"Because," said Raggedy Ann as she made her magic scooter hop over a log which lay in her path, "because Dinkie told us that he had been sent by the Magician to stop us so we would not rescue Ted's mama and daddy."

So, laughing and talking, the friends rode along the path through the deep, deep woods. Suddenly, and without the least warning, Raggedy Ann and little Ted came to a sudden stop. And behind them Raggedy Andy also came to a sudden stop and they all fell on the ground together. Grampy Hoppytoad fell down too, but fortunately he and little Ted landed on the soft Raggedys so they were not hurt. Gilly Imp and the Bugaboo, riding way behind, were able to stop in time and helped the others to their feet.

"Do you suppose the magic has gone out of the scooters?" Raggedy Andy asked.

"Oh no, Raggedy Andy," Raggedy Ann said. "The scooters ran into an invisible wall. I'm sure that is what stopped us so suddenly."

"That must be it," Grampy Hoppytoad said. "The Magician has made a magic invisible wall so that we cannot pass."

"Now we shall never be able to find my nice mama and daddy!" little Ted said, and he looked very sad.

Raggedy Ann put her soft, floppy arms around the little boy and said, "Never fear, we shall find a way to rescue your mama and daddy."

"I know what to do," Raggedy Andy said. "I shall get on my magic scooter and ride it toward the invisible wall. Then, when I come to it, I shall make the magic scooter hop right up over the wall."

Everyone thought this would be a fine idea, so Raggedy Andy took his scooter way back to get a good start. Then he rode, lickety-split, toward the invisible wall. And then he lifted the scooter up into the air.

It looked to the others as though Raggedy Andy's scooter would carry him right up and over. But when the scooter was way up in the air, it went "Bump" and hit against the invisible wall.

Both the scooter and Raggedy Andy came tumbling down to the ground. Gilly Imp and the Bugaboo helped Raggedy Andy to his feet and put the scooter upright.

WORTH GRUELLE

"It didn't hurt a bit." Raggedy Andy laughed as he brushed the dirt from his shirt. "But the invisible wall is very high. I shall try again and this time, I shall send the scooter higher into the air."

Raggedy Ann had been sitting and thinking, and she thought so hard that she ripped a stitch out of her rag head.

Suddenly she said, "Maybe the invisible wall is even higher than you think. Next time, you may jump your magic scooter right into it, and break the scooter."

"What else can I do?" asked Raggedy Andy.

"Hmmm," his little rag doll friend said. "Try riding your scooter up the side of the invisible wall and when you reach the top, stop the scooter. Then we can all follow you and slide down the other side together."

So Raggedy Andy rode his magic scooter clear to the top of the invisible wall which was, indeed, higher than anyone had thought it could be.

"Come on," he called down as he stopped the scooter at the top and waited for the others.

So Raggedy Ann, little Ted, Grampy Hoppytoad, Gilly Imp and the Bugaboo rode up to the top. They all slid down together, and nobody was bumped at all.

When they reached the ground on the other side, Grampy Hoppytoad put on his magic green spectacles. Then he could once more see the footprints of little Ted's mama, leading down the path toward a bush covered with crisp, brown pretzels.

Everyone rode his scooter to the pretzel bush,

and next to it they found a ginger-ale spring which sparkled in the sunshine. The ginger ale and pretzels made a delightful snack while they rested.

They decided that they must follow the footprints. Perhaps they would lead them to the Magician himself. Then they would try to persuade the Magician to release little Ted's sweet mama and daddy. So they rode along for a while, wondering how much farther they would have to go before they came to the Magician's house.

All at once, something struck Raggedy Andy squarely on the head and knocked him off his scooter so he fell head over heels on the ground. Then something struck Raggedy Ann and she fell head over heels. In another moment, all the others had been hit.

Little Ted ran and hid in a hollow tree while Grampy Hoppytoad ran away through the bushes at the side of the path. Gilly Imp and the Bugaboo ran to protect the Raggedys but as soon as they stood up, they were knocked down again. And the same thing happened to both the Raggedys.

When they had been knocked down more times than they could count, Raggedy Ann said, "I guess we shall have to find a place to hide, because these blows are coming too thick and fast. And we cannot even see where they are coming from."

So the Raggedys crawled to the tree where little Ted was safely hidden and got in beside him. Gilly Imp and the Bugaboo hid in another tree near by. They all watched through holes in the trees. And finally Raggedy Ann said, "I guess the Magician must have made a magic cannon!"

Now they could see yellow cannon balls coming through the air. Following with their eyes, they could see the yellow balls coming from high in the air.

Raggedy Ann shouted, "I see, I see. The yellow cannon balls are coming from the top of the Magician's castle up there!"

The yellow cannon balls were coming thicker and faster now and it was very fortunate that the Raggedys and all their friends were safely hidden.

"I hope they haven't captured Grampy Hoppytoad," whispered Raggedy Andy. "He might be very frightened out there all by himself."

Raggedy Ann looked out of the hole in the tree and then said, "They have stopped shooting the cannon balls. I guess they think they have conquered us. Maybe they are coming to capture us."

Raggedy Andy said, "But maybe they will not find us if we stay here in the tree and remain quiet."

Presently they could hear the tramp, tramp, tramp of many feet and they were indeed worried. But they kept very, very quiet. Then, as the tramping grew louder and louder and came close to their hiding place, they heard the voice of Grampy Hoppytoad.

He called out, "Oh, Raggedy Ann, Raggedy Andy, where are you?"

Thinking that they must try to help their old friend, they jumped out of the tree. And then they burst into laughter. For there was Grampy Hoppytoad, marching at the head of a group of little soldiers who looked so scared they seemed about to cry.

Grampy proudly explained, "I slipped behind them after they left the castle, and I croaked so hard, they were frightened and started running back. They thought I was magic, so they came along and have done all that I told them to! Let's stop here and rest, for I am tired after that hard work," said Grampy Hoppytoad with a wink.

So Raggedy Ann and Raggedy Andy and all the others sat down to rest. And they ate some beautiful oranges which were growing on a tree not far away.

"Now, let's see." Raggedy Ann thought out loud.

"The Magician sent his soldiers to capture us. But Grampy Hoppytoad has captured them instead."

Just then Gilly Imp smashed his hand upon his knee and exclaimed, "I know just what we can do! We can have the soldiers lead us right to the Magician and they can capture him for us!"

His friend the Bugaboo became so excited that he shouted, "Then the Magician will have to set little Ted's mama and daddy free!"

"Hooray, Hooray!" shouted little Ted. "I think Raggedy Andy ought to be the new Captain for the soldiers. He will make them mind well."

The others readily agreed to this. So the little rag doll stood tall and straight in front of the shaking soldiers and gave his orders.

"You will march straight to the castle and lead us to the Magician himself! Then you will take him prisoner immediately!"

Without a word, the soldiers lined up and began marching through the woods. The others followed slowly on their magic scooters singing merrily.

Suddenly, Raggedy Andy called, "Halt!"

The soldiers stopped instantly and then Raggedy Andy ordered, "Capture that man!"

And the soldiers grabbed poor Dinkie who was trying to hide under some bushes.

Once more they went ahead, and soon the castle was in sight. It was a huge building but the door was just an old wooden one. So Raggedy Andy bravely marched up to it, and knocked, *knock! knock! knock!* just as easily as that.

CHAPTER 9

THE OLD WOODEN door opened slowly. There stood a little old stooped-over woman with white hair hanging down her back, her clothes in tatters. Raggedy Andy stepped back for she was indeed ugly!

But when she spoke, her voice and words were pleasant. "Come in quickly please—I have been waiting for you. Take this to help you." And she handed Raggedy Andy a shining sword.

Raggedy Andy was surprised, but took the sword for he thought he might need it. Then, with Raggedy Ann at one side, and little Ted at his other side, he marched into the castle, followed by the frightened soldiers. After them came Grampy Hoppytoad, Gilly Imp and the Bugaboo. They had offered to march at the back to make sure the soldiers would follow Raggedy Andy's orders.

The old woman led them right through a huge hall to a room where they saw a very tall man. And they knew that he was the Magician.

Raggedy Andy stepped forward and was about

to say politely, "Good day," but the Magician spoke first.

"What do you want?" the Magician asked rudely.

So Raggedy Andy tipped his hat politely and replied, "I want to find little Ted's nice mama and daddy."

At this, the Magician laughed very loudly, "Ha, Ha, Ha!"

Then he put on his eyeglasses and looked at Raggedy Andy over the tops.

"So you are Raggedy Andy, are you?" the Magician asked.

Raggedy Andy could only nod his head up and down.

Then the Magician poked Raggedy Andy with his cane and pushed the rag doll over on his back.

"Ha, ha, ha!" The Magician laughed. "I could fight you as easy as pie if I wanted to. I can't understand why my soldiers let you capture them."

"Then I shall tell you, Mister Magician," Raggedy Andy said as he got to his feet and brushed off his clothes. "The reason why it was so easy to conquer your soldiers was because I am fighting for little Ted's nice mama and daddy. The soldiers were only fighting for a mean old Magician. And anyone fighting for the right and good thing can fight ten times as well as someone fighting for the wrong or bad thing."

Raggedy Andy stood as tall and straight as he could and his friends were very proud of him.

"Ha!" the Magician cried, and Raggedy Andy

could see that he was very angry. "Just for that, Mister Raggedy Andy, you and I shall have a fight."

So the Magician took off his hat and began to roll up his sleeves, getting ready to fight Raggedy Andy.

"Hmmm!" thought Raggedy Andy to himself. "Why should I wait for the Magician to get ready to fight me when he is so much larger than I? I shall start right now!"

So Raggedy Andy did just that. He whacked the Magician on top of his head with the flat side of the sword which the ugly old lady had given him. Then he smacked the Magician on his back hard with the sword. And each time the Magician howled loudly.

"Just wait until I get ready, will you, Mister Raggedy Andy?" he screamed.

But Raggedy Andy just kept right on thumping and smacking the Magician on all sides until the mean old Magician felt all black and blue. And seeing that Raggedy Andy was getting the better of him the Magician took to his heels and flew out of the castle as fast as he could.

"Ha, ha, ha!" Raggedy Ann and all the others

laughed, for they had been watching with great interest. "Raggedy Andy won the fight as easy as pie!"

"But now that Raggedy Andy has fought the wicked Magician and sent him off howling, I am afraid the Magician will begin to work magic on you as he did on me," the white-haired old lady said as she came in from the kitchen.

With her she brought some ice cream for Raggedy Andy to eat as he sat and rested after the fight.

"No, I believe now that the Magician knows what a good fighter Raggedy Andy is he will not try to stop us," Grampy Hoppytoad said.

Raggedy Ann said, "Just as soon as Raggedy Andy has rested, we shall search the Magician's castle and rescue little Ted's nice mama and daddy."

"Oh, I do wish you could make the Magician change me back to what I used to be," the poor white-haired old lady sobbed. "Just see what a long, ugly nose the Magician gave me. I was really much prettier before the Magician made me so ugly."

"That just shows we must never judge anyone by the way he looks," Raggedy Ann said. "Here is an ugly woman, made ugly by a wicked Magician, but inside she is very lovely. Indeed, we shall try our best to make the Magician change you back into the pretty lady you once were."

"Now we are ready to find the Magician," Raggedy Andy said as he picked up his long sharp sword.

Even though the mean old Magician had been beaten in his fight with Raggedy Andy, he did not intend to let the Raggedys and their friends find little

Ted's mama and daddy if he could help it. He was hiding in the bushes right outside the castle, thinking about Raggedy Andy. He thought and thought for a long, long time until he had an idea.

"Ah," he thought to himself, "I know what! When I sent my soldiers to fight Raggedy Andy, they became frightened. I shall have to send some magical thing which cannot think or get scared; then it is sure to overcome Raggedy Andy and his friends."

So the Magician got out some of his charms and made many large yellow pumpkins. There were sixteen of them altogether.

"Aha!" He laughed out loud. "Now there are enough large pumpkins to roll over the Raggedys and all their friends and squash them flat! Then they will have to crawl home—if they can still crawl!"

So the Magician took the sixteen large pumpkins out into the path. He waved his magic wand over them and said, "Now then, magic pumpkins, I want you to roll right smack at Raggedy Andy and knock him down and roll right on top of him. That will roll him out flat as a pancake and he will not be able to fight. Then I shall come along behind you and send Raggedy Andy scooting for home."

"Now remember," he said severely to the pumpkins, "do not turn aside for anything at all. Roll right smack straight at Raggedy Andy, for he is very brave and smart and will try his best to fool you."

With that, the Magician started the large pumpkins rolling down the path and into the castle. Raggedy Ann was the first to hear the pumpkins.

87

"Blumpity! Blump! Blumpity!" they came, sounding like distant thunder as they rolled along.

"The Magician is sending something magical to make us leave," said Raggedy Ann to the others.

"What makes you think that?" asked Grampy Hoppytoad. "It sounds like thunder to me, that's all!"

"Just wait and you will see," said Raggedy Ann.

So they stood still and in a few minutes they could see the sixteen large magical pumpkins come through the castle door and roll straight toward them.

"Oh me!" cried little Ted. "The Magician has sent those magical pumpkins to roll on us and squash us flat. Whatever shall we do?"

"Everyone get behind me," cried Raggedy Andy. "And everyone brace the one in front of him."

So Raggedy Ann stood behind Raggedy Andy and braced him, then Grampy Hoppytoad came behind Raggedy Ann. And little Ted stood behind Grampy Hoppytoad, while behind the litle boy were Gilly Imp, the little old lady, and the Bugaboo.

Raggedy Andy stood perfectly still until the first pumpkin was within a few feet of him. Then the little rag doll, standing tall and straight, raised his sharp sword and held it straight out ahead of him.

Now the magical pumpkins rolled straight toward Raggedy Andy as the Magician had told them. They rolled straight into Raggedy Andy's sword and were cut right in two! And each half went rolling to one side without even touching the Raggedys or their friends.

WORTH GRUELLE

CHAPTER 10

OF COURSE, the Magician could not see what was happening to the pumpkins inside the castle, but he was quite sure they would obey his magic commands. So, whistling cheerily, he skipped back to the castle and ran into the room where the Raggedys were. And just as the last of the sixteen pumpkins had waddled away, the Magician came along.

"Now I shall find Raggedy Andy squashed as flat as a pancake!" he thought to himself and chuckled.

But when he saw his magical pumpkins cut in two and Raggedy Andy standing there with his long sharp sword, the Magician thought, "My goodness! I shall not stay here and be captured!

So he turned and was about to run away as fast as his scared feet could carry him.

"Ha, ha, ha," Raggedy Andy laughed, seeing the look on the Magician's face. "You thought you would find squashed Raggedys! Now you had better stand still and do as I say!"

And the Magician thought this was the best thing

89

to do, for Raggedy Andy was even stronger than the Magician thought he could be.

"What do you want, Mister Raggedy Andy?" the Magician asked, just as if he did not know that the Raggedys had come there to rescue little Ted's mama and daddy.

"We want you to free little Ted's nice mama and daddy, and also to change this poor old lady back into a nice pretty young woman," Raggedy Andy said.

"Aha! So that is what you wish!" the Magician cried as if he had not known it all the time. "Well, I shall not do it, that's all!"

"Then we shall see!" cried Raggedy Andy, though he did not really know yet what he would do.

"What will you do? Just tell me that, Mister Raggedy Andy!" the Magician said, as mean as could be.

"I'll cut off your nose, and I'll cut off your ears!" Raggedy Andy promised.

"Dear me! I shouldn't like that at all!" The Magician shuddered. But pretending that he was very brave, he said, "I shall not do as you ask unless you bring me the golden canary with the diamond eyes."

"There isn't any such thing." Raggedy Andy laughed.

"Ha, ha, ha, I know that." The Magician laughed loudly. "You'll have to find one then."

Just then Grampy Hoppytoad hopped over to Raggedy Andy and whispered something into his ear.

Raggedy Andy smiled and turned to the Magician. "We shall not have to bother with you. The soldiers here will guard you in this room while we search the

rest of the castle to find little Ted's mama and daddy."

Then he added sharply, "Dinkie here will lead us in our search of the castle."

"Anyway," Raggedy Andy said as they started their search, "we have captured the Magician and his castle, even if we cannot make the Magician do as we say."

So with Dinkie leading the way, upstairs, downstairs and all over, the Raggedys and the others searched all through the Magician's castle. But nowhere could they find little Ted's mama and daddy.

The Magician had a very fine castle. There were many wonderful things that the Magician had taken away from other people. And there was a magical soda-water fountain and some lollypop plants.

So the Raggedys and their friends ate ice-cream cones from the magical kitchen while they searched all over. Then Raggedy Ann, Raggedy Andy and Grampy Hoppytoad decided they must get the Magician's magic charms so that he would be powerless. Then he would have to free little Ted's mama and daddy.

Calling Dinkie to her, Raggedy Ann said kindly, "We would like to be your friends, Dinkie. And we think that if you were our friend too we could all have a lot of fun together."

And Grampy Hoppytoad chimed in, "Doing the right thing is really fun, and it makes you feel ever so good all over, Dinkie."

To their surprise, Dinkie burst into tears and

sobbed, "I never really liked the Magician! And it truly isn't much fun doing scary things. I would like to be your friend, if you will let me."

Raggedy Ann wiped Dinkie's tears away, and Gilly Imp whispered, "That was what we found out too, Dinkie. Bugaboo and I are glad that we became friends of the Raggedys."

The little fat man shyly asked, "Do you think I could ever have a golden ring like Mr. Carpenter and Gilly Imp and the Bugaboo?"

Raggedy Andy assured the little fat man, "If you prove to have a kind, generous heart."

A smile appeared on Dinkie's round face and he said, "My, I have so many important things to do. First, I shall show you where all the Magician's really strong charms are. When you have those, the Magician will have to free little Ted's mama and daddy."

Running to a tiny door under the window, Dinkie called to Raggedy Andy, "Here they are!"

Dinkie, being the Magician's Messenger, knew how to open the door and he had done this by the time Raggedy Andy reached it. The little rag doll spread a large hankie on the floor and put all the magic charms in it. Then he tied the four corners of the hankie into a knot and put it on his shoulder.

The little band of friends marched together to the room where the Magician was still held prisoner by his own soldiers. The Magician, seeing them all come through the doorway, wondered what Raggedy Andy could be carrying. But he soon knew what it was.

Raggedy Andy put the hankie down on the floor

and spread it open. Then he stood up and looked straight at the Magician, without saying a word.

When the mean Magician saw all his powerful charms collected on the floor, he looked at his soldiers, but they would not help him. He cried out, "Now I have lost all my magic! Oh me, Oh my!"

Raggedy Andy said sternly, "If you do not free little Ted's mama and daddy, I shall cut off your long nose with my sword."

Of course the Magician did not see Raggedy Andy wink his eye, for the rag doll was really too kind-hearted to cut off anyone's nose.

"Ted's mama has been with you all the time," the Magician cried as he pointed to the ugly old woman with the white hair.

But little Ted cried, "That is not how my nice, pretty sweet mother looked!"

Raggedy Andy took his sword and held it over the Magician's head as he exclaimed, "Now use your magic to change little Ted's mama back the way she used to be! Hurry!"

Trembling, the Magician danced around the hankie holding his magic charms as he said these words:

> "One, two, three, four,
>   Magic charms upon the floor.
>   Let little Ted's mama be
>   Pretty and young for all to see.
>   Set little Ted's daddy free
>   So he may with them be.
>   Hocus, pocus! Abacadabra!"

94

Before their eyes, the ugly old woman changed into a pretty young lady. She ran to little Ted and hugged and kissed him, weeping with happiness.

And a sad-looking soldier standing near Raggedy Andy became a handsome, tall man who flew to the side of little Ted and his mother and embraced them.

So now everyone was happy and gay. Even the Magician had to smile at all the happiness around him and he decided it might be fun to be kind to people. He invited the Raggedys and their friends to stay with him in his castle and be his guests.

Little Ted's mama and Raggedy Ann went into the kitchen and prepared a huge dinner in no time with the help of the magic charms.

Then it was time for the Raggedys to say good-by to all their friends. As the Raggedys left the castle, each with an arm about the other, they found two lovely trees on either side of the old wooden door.

Each tree had many boughs heavy with beautiful golden rings. And the rings, swaying gently in the breeze, seemed to sing softly, "Happy Adventures, Raggedy Ann! Happy Adventures, Raggedy Andy!"

THE
GRUELLE IDEAL

It is the Gruelle ideal
that books for children
should contain nothing to
cause fright, suggest fear, glo-
rify mischief, excuse malice
or condone cruelty. That
is why they are called
"BOOKS GOOD FOR
CHILDREN."